NOT MY SON

An Urban Short Story

EBONY Q.

Copyright © 2023 by Q.E. Publishing (Ebony Q.)

ISBN 979-8-9887343-1-4

All rights reserved.

No part of this book may be reproduced in any form or by any electronic or mechanical means, including information storage and retrieval systems, without written permission from the author, except for the use of brief quotations in a book review.

Cover Design by LaMar Hall.

This is a work of fiction. Names, characters, places, and incidents either are the product of the author's imagination or are used fictitiously. Any resemblance to actual persons, living or dead, events, or locales is entirely coincidental.

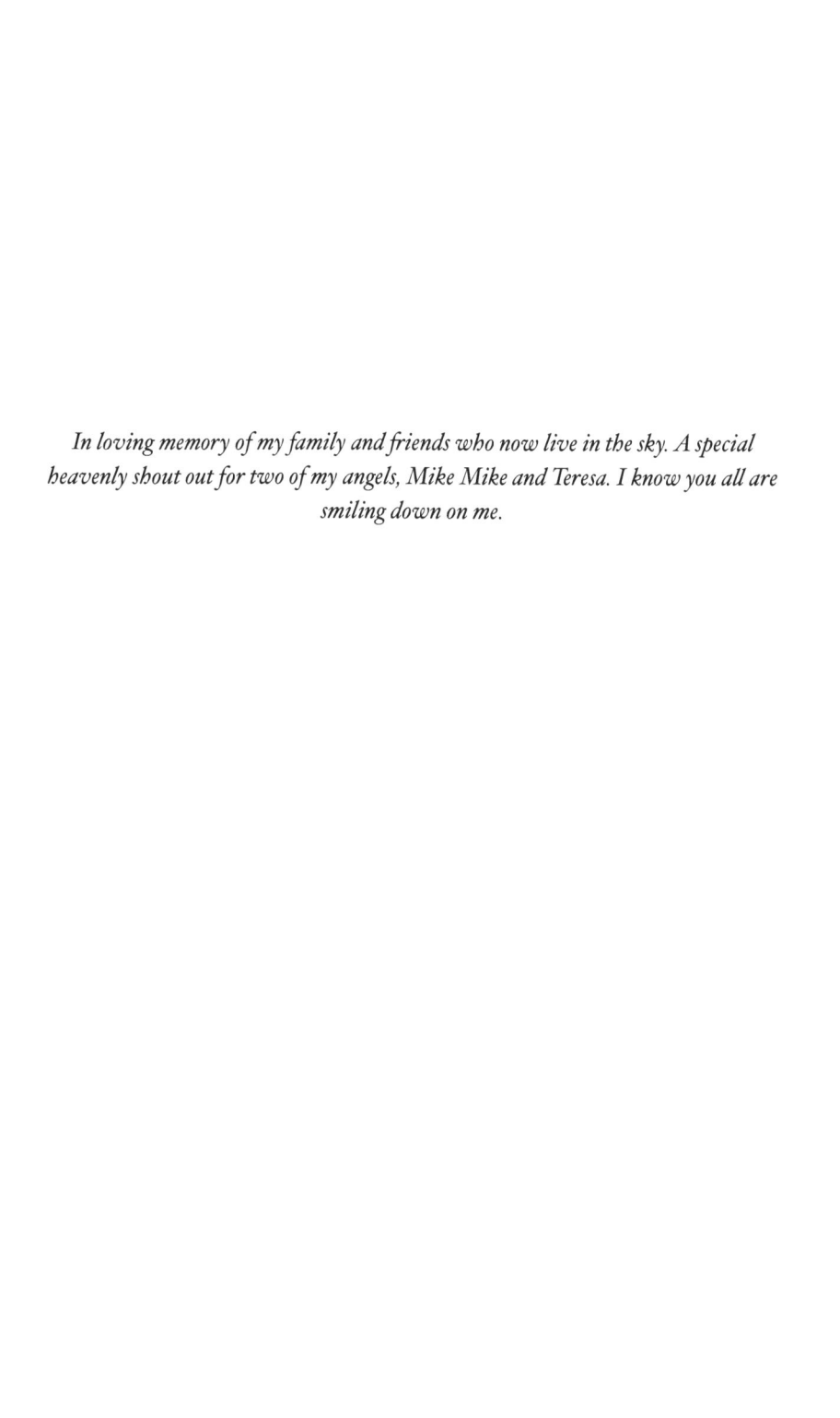

In loving memory of my family and friends who now live in the sky. A special heavenly shout out for two of my angels, Mike Mike and Teresa. I know you all are smiling down on me.

ACKNOWLEDGMENTS

Lord you made this possible. Thank you for blessing me with the gift and the vision. You're so amazing in my life.

I'm thankful to my family and friends for your support. I'm forever grateful to my test readers Divine, Dennis (the professor) and Michelle. I appreciate you giving your time to support my project. Kaneka, my muse, thanks for being there for me...literally, every day. Thank you to everyone on my launch team, who read my book in advance—I can't thank you enough. Quineshia, thanks for sharing your insight and experience, and listening to me talk non-stop.

Huge shout-out and thanks to my book trailer crew for sharing your talent: Divine, Mary, Demetrio, Chey, Robert, Connor, Starr and Jane. I'll never forget that day.

Finally, I'm thankful to my husband and son for your help, support & love.

Thank you everyone for joining me on my journey. This means everything to me. I'm overwhelmed with gratitude.

~

To every parent that says, "My child would never ..."

PLAYLIST

Songs that inspired the characters & story

My Life by Mary J. Blige
Knuck If You Buck by Crime Mob
DontGetIt by Lil Wayne
Whatta Man by Salt-N-Pepa (feat. En Vogue)
Bout It, Bout It II by Master P
Weak by SWV
Who Want the Smoke by Lil Yachty (feat. Cardi B & Offset)
No Ordinary Love by Sade
*I Don't F**k With You* by Big Sean (feat. E-40)
Sorry by Beyoncé
Tha Crossroads by Bone Thugs-n-Harmony
Hot Boy by Nardo Wick (feat. Lil Baby)
The Boss by Rick Ross (feat. T-Pain)
Killing Me Softly With His song by Fugees
Goodbye Love by Guy
Cry for You by Jodeci
Need U Bad by Jazmine Sullivan

MAJESTY
Drama

"You need to come get Divine, he's done something to Legend's puppy."

"What? I don't have time for your jokes Majesty."

"Elegance, does it sound like I'm joking?"

"I'm at work, what you want me to do?"

"You heard me. I want you to come get him."

"We all want something in life that's not going to happen."

I hear the aggravation in my sister's voice. *Let me hurry up and end this call before I snap on her.* "We're headed to Grandma's house," I ignore her comment.

"Whatever. Bye."

I hope my baby's puppy is ok. Jayvon and Legend rushed him to the vet. I hurried Divine out my house to get him away from Jayvon and the chaos he's caused. Divine and I ride in silence to my Grandmother's house. I glance in the rearview mirror at my nephew. He's looking out the window, nodding to whatever rapper is rhyming to him through his AirPods. The light breeze flowing in the cracked windows is soothing. I hope it pulls the odor from the back seat out the windows. I don't want it lingering in my car. It came with Divine and needs to leave with his funky ass.

EBONY Q.

My sister needs to do something with this boy. Her current method ain't working. All she does is deny, defend, and dismiss. I love her and my nephew but his behavior is starting to worry me. It worries everyone except her.

Fifteen minutes later we arrive at our destination.

"Hey Grandma, we're here."

"Hey baby." Grandma hugs me then Divine. "Hey boy."

"Hey Grandma Wanda." Divine says before disappearing to the back of the house.

"Rest yourself and tell me what's going on." Grandma directs me to the sofa.

I explain how Legend rushed in the room to Jayvon and I—hysterical. His face is full of tears, his chest heaving up and down and his words hard to understand. Legend saw Divine giving the puppy something to drink. Divine rushed to leave out when Legend entered. Legend said the puppy walked with wobbly legs, like Bambi. Then it collapsed, started shaking and started vomiting. When we rushed into the room the puppy was seizing and foaming out the mouth.

"Mmm Mmm Mmm." Grandma shakes her head. "What his mama say?"

"Nothing really."

"Baby, I don't know why she won't believe nobody but him."

"Exacty. The crazy thing is he acted like nothing was wrong. He denied it of course."

"Who you telling? I know he did."

"I'm starting to worry about him."

"Starting? I've known for years something ain't right with him."

"For years?" I question. "Granny, he's only 13."

"Chile, for about 7 - 8 years now. Ever since he was young. You know what I'm trying to say."

She's right. Elegance has been told countless times of things Divine has done or said that are disturbing. Things most would consider red flags for a child.

"You know why he do it, don't you?"

"Why Granny?"

"Cuz Ele don't do nothing. This new age parenting got these kids all messed up. The good book say spare the rod and spoil the child."

"Granny, she won't spank him. She might fuss (and that's heavy on the might), then she rewards him."

"Chile, you ain't telling me nothing I don't know. I can tell how you parent by how your child behave. That boy don't have no fear of nothing. You mark my words, before long she will fear him."

"Why you say that?"

"I feel it in my spirit. She wanna raise him as a friend. She may be his friend but he's *not* her friend."

"What can we do to help?"

"Nothing! We can't do nothing. You can't raise other people chirren, especially if they don't want your help. Ele don't want the help."

"I've tried a million different ways to convince her."

"You go on but I ain't in the business of wasting my time. I rather watch my shows, especially my favorite judge." Granny slapped her knee and starting laughing.

"He's too young for you."

"Hush your mouth, child. I can look. I'm old, not blind. I like him cuz he don't play. You can tell he was raised old school."

"Woman, what am I gonna do with you?"

Granny blushed, "Nothing. You can't do nothing with me cuz I'm full grown, been grown."

"I'm stuck with you and you're stuck with me."

"Maj - I was kidding around," Granny says before getting serious. "You keep telling Ele what she needs to hear. I know you get tired but keep at it anyhow. You hear me?"

I nod in agreement.

"See, in order for plants to grow you gotta nourish them. You gotta provide the nutrients. You give 'em water. Sometimes the soil may not be ready so the water don't go nowhere. It sits on top. After while the soil will absorb the water. It'll get down in there. Mmm Hmm."

"Yes Ma'am."

"Mmm Hmm, that's what I know. She ain't ready yet, but don't grow weary, child.

In due time.

BUT, if she keeps turning a blind eye, she's gonna learn the hard way."

CLICK CLICK

We direct our attention to the front door as it's unlocked.

"Chile, I hope you're ready for what's about to walk in."

ELEGANCE

Truth

"Hey Gran Gran." I hug and kiss my second mother.
"Hey Sugar."
"Majesty." I throw side eye to Ms. Goody-Goody.
"Elegance," she frowned.

I sit across from them to face the trash about to come my way. "What's up? I left work early to come over here." I ask looking at my big sister. "What has he done (I make air quotes) now?" *I'm so tired of her bullshit. She always overreacts.*

Majesty rolls her eyes. "Like I said on the phone," Majesty begins, "Divine did something to Legend's puppy."

I suck my teeth. "What? Naw, Divine loves animals."

"Legend saw him giving the dog something to drink then the dog damn near passed out."

"And y'all know Divine did something?"

"Legend saw him do it."

"So automatically *my* son is lying cuz ain't no way *your* son is lying."

"If I had to pick which one was lying, I'm gonna say Divine is lying," Gran said. "I love both of them and both of y'all, but don't act like he's an angel."

"I never said he was an angel," I snap.

Majesty snapped at me, "Don't take that tone with Granny."

"I'm sorry Gran," I look in her direction. "You have no idea how tired I am of people always trying to blame stuff on Divine."

"And why do you think that is, baby?"

"I don't know but it's getting old."

"I'm not people. I'm his aunt. I love you both and you know that. Elegance, be real. Why would we make this up? Legend broke down crying, damn near hyperventilating."

He's overreacting like his Mama. He get it from his Mama. I roll my eyes and smirk.

"I'm glad you think this is funny while you're over there rolling your eyes?"

"Who hyperventilates over a damn dog? Just saying." I smirk at her. "What's this really about? A damn vet bill?"

"This is about the disturbing things your son does and how you never do anything about it."

"I raise my child my way. You raise your child your way."

"What are you going to do, Ele?"

I shrug. "I don't even know if he did this."

"You heard Maj," Gran said.

"I don't know if I believe that. Maybe Jayvon made all this up because he really don't want Divine over there anymore."

"Something is wrong with you," Majesty said. "Now that's a lie that even you don't believe. Jayvon is a concerned uncle and doesn't want the bad behavior of his nephew, whom he loves, to rub off on his son."

"Yeah, sure."

"Elegance you said yourself that Darvin has concern about Divine's behavior too."

I roll my eyes. "That was months ago. They're like besties now." *Actually, they're not. We may break up soon because he keeps saying stuff about Divine and it's getting old.*

"I hear y'all talking about me," Divine says.

We all direct our attention to the back of the room where Divine had slipped in unnoticed.

"Hey, Boo." I greet my only child.

"Hey, Ma."

"You're not going to address what he said to us?" Majesty is fuming.

I ignore her. "Did you do something to Legend's puppy?"

"Nope. I was playing with him but then he started acting weird."

"What did you give him?" Majesty asked.

"Who?"

"Divine, don't play with me."

"Don't do that, Majesty." I say defending my son.

"I'm not auntie." He looked up to the left. "I told you I didn't do nothing."

"Baby, go back in the back room." Gran directed.

Divine disappeared as fast as he'd come.

"That boy's lying." Gran said. "You believe what you wanna Ele, but ain't no truth in what he said."

"How do you know?"

"I ain't get old by being a fool. He looked everywhere but at us. Plus, he was too calm. He ain't fuss enough trying to prove hisself."

"Mmm Hmm." Majesty adds.

"It's a shame that your own family be the ones trying to bring you down. Family should be safe." *I'm not surprised Gran is taking her side.*

"Safe," Majesty shrieks. "I don't feel safe with your son around, especially not around my son."

"Now, that's the realest thing you've said all day."

"Ele, you can't get upset with your sister. She ain't telling you nothing to hurt you."

"I don't know Gran."

"Oh, I don't believe this." Majesty huffs.

"Ele, he may be struggling with some spiritual warfare." Gran continued. "You can't deny what's in his blood from his daddy side of the family."

"Right, generational curses." Majesty said. "He gets it honest but there are resources available."

"I don't need you being a principal right now," I roll my eyes.

"Cut it out Ele. That girl ain't say nothing out the way," Gran corrected me.

"Mama never wanted you to get mixed up with them," Majesty reminded.

"Baby, that whole family been crazy. You hear me? Huh?" Gran continued. "I been knowing them and they all got issues." Gran pointed at her temple with her index finger while rotating it in a circular motion. "Diana was so upset when you got pregnant by that fool."

"Gran, you're not supposed to call people fools. Is that Christian?" I ask half serious, half joking.

"It's the truth. The Lord knows it." Gran chuckles.

"If y'all are so convinced that Divine is dealing with stuff because of his dad's side, y'all have a funny way of showing it." I look back and forth between the two of them. "Y'all ain't giving him no kind of breaks."

"He gets enough breaks from you," Majesty said. "It's called tough love."

"Ele, she's right," Gran said.

Of course she is. "DIVINE," I holler for him. "I'm tired and we don't see eye to eye on this."

"What are you going to do?" Majesty prodded.

"I'm gonna raise my son how *I* see fit. If that's alright with you."

"Whatever, do you." Majesty sounded annoyed.

"I always do." I leave the room to go get Divine from the back.

"What are you doing?" I ask Divine as he walks out of Gran's bedroom.

"Nothing, I'm ready to go."

"Why are you in her room?"

"I dropped my AirPod and it rolled in there." He shrugged.

"C'mon let's go."

I can hear Gran and Majesty talking as I get closer to the living room. They stop as soon as they see us.

"Alright Gran, we're leaving now. I love you."

"I love you too sugar. Think about what we talked about."

"I will," I lie and give Gran a hug.

"Give your grandma a hug and tell her bye," I tell Divine. He ignores me and walks to the door.

"I don't feel like hugging. I'm tired. Can you hurry up?" He walks out the door.

"He's had a long day, especially with all this going on."

"Stop making excuses for him, Elegance. You know that's not cool to let him talk to you like that." Majesty looks at me.

"Ele, if you keep ignoring the signs and making excuses for him, you'll be doing it his whole life. Until there comes a time when you can't anymore" Gran emphasized.

It's taking everything in me not to roll my eyes at Gran.

I had no way of knowing how true Gran's words were.

MAJESTY

Listen

"Are you convinced now? Is this enough?" Jayvon asked.
They'd finally made it home. The puppy had to stay at the vet. He's in critical condition. *For my baby's sake, I hope he survives.*

"I get it," I tell my sexy husband.

"Do you Maj," he questioned. "I'm not convinced." He leans back against our padded headboard, interlocking his fingers behind his head.

"Jay, I'm...I'm scared. On the drive to Grandma's, Divine looked carefree. He wasn't scared or nervous."

"Your sister needs to get him help before it's too late."

"Don't say that."

"It's the truth. He poisoned our puppy. We don't know if Rocky is going to survive, and if he does, will he have issues?"

"If only Elegance will let me help her. There are so many resources available."

"Love, I know it's in your nature to try to help kids. This is different."

"Right, it is different because it's family."

"No, Divine is your nephew, not your son. Your son is upset about his puppy and why his cousin tried to hurt him. Divine is your sister's issue."

I know my nephew needs help, but I want to be a part of the support group for him. I can't leave him hanging. I don't know if I can keep my promise about keeping my distance from my nephew.

"It's bad that Legend knows Divine did something to hurt Rocky."

Jayvon nodded in agreement. "Love, we can't allow Divine to cause chaos over here. His behavior is getting worse."

"You're right baby. You should have heard how he was talking back to Elegance. Granny said we need to be careful." *That might be taking it a little too far.*

Jayvon pulled me into his bare chest. I love when he wraps me up in his embrace. It had been a source of comfort for me since our college days. "It's my job to protect and provide for this family. I won't let anything happen to you all. I don't want Legend going to their house. Truth be told, I don't want Divine back over here. I know that's not going to happen. He can come here but Legend can't go over there without us. You know your sister won't keep an eye on them."

"I wish Divine had a positive, loving father in his life."

"Speaking of his father, I don't understand why Elegance doesn't put Divine in counseling. Especially after what his father did to that poor woman."

"She doesn't believe in mental health providers or seeking professional help. She defends him, so we don't talk about it."

"That's a problem. What does that boy have to do to make her get him help?"

"I don't know what it will take, maybe nothing."

"It's going to take his path of destruction coming to her front door."

ELEGANCE
Deny

I roll my eyes. They need to hurry up. I'm not going to sit here and wait forever. I just dealt with Majesty and her foolishness with the dog and a week later, now this. Hell, I had to leave work to come over here. I'm so sick of these people. They're so extra.

The only reason I wasn't raising hell yet was because that fine ass cop kept walking by. He might be my next boo. It was something about a man in uniform that did it for me. It's clear he likes how these scrubs were fitting me. He was eyeing me as much as I was checking him out.

"Right this way, Principal James is ready now."

"It's about time," I snap.

"Good afternoon, come on in." Principal James motioned for me to enter her office. I maintained a stone face. My gut tells me this is about to be some bullshit when I notice a file on her desk with Divine's name on it.

I've been in this woman's office 50 million times. I'm tired of seeing her raggedy diplomas on the wall behind her desk. I'm sick of seeing her ugly family photos on her bookshelf, especially the one with the dumb dog wearing a bandana. I'm over the view of the parking lot from the window in here. Each time I come, I'm bothered by the monitors with the various camera displays of the school. It seems like an invasion of privacy to watch people all the time. Did anyone consent to this? I know I didn't.

"Ms. Patterson, there's no easy way to say this," she began. "Divine set a small fire in the restroom today."

"How do you know it was him?" *I have to defend my baby because they ALWAYS want to blame him, like he's the only one that does things.*

"We're certain it's him because it's captured on camera. The video shows him going in the restroom with his backpack (which violates school policy). He's in there for 15 minutes, then runs out."

"Was anyone hurt? Any damage?" I ask.

"Fortunately, no one was hurt and there was only minor damage. The plastic trashcan was burned." She pulls some papers out of the file and places it in front of me.

"What's this?" I motion to the papers.

These papers were found in the bathroom. She points at the top of each paper. Each one has Divine's handwritten name on it. She explains they believe he used paper from his backpack to start the fire. She goes on to say they searched his bag and found a lighter in there.

"I must have accidentally dropped my lighter in his bag when I was signing some papers for him." *That sounds good. I study her face to see if she's buying my made-up story.*

"If that's true, you should be more careful. You don't want to accidentally catch charges for contributing to the delinquency of a minor," she smirked.

Fuck her. I see her grinning. She won't be laughing when I call the school board on her.

I ask, "Is something funny?"

"Of course not. This is no laughing matter." She retrieves more documents from the file. "Do you remember these?"

I look at the new stack of papers she's put on display.

Fighting.

Bullying.

Tardiness.

Threatening a student.

Vandalism.

Disrupting class.

Defiance to a teacher.
Destroying school property.
Bus Suspensions.

All of these are write-ups they did on Divine. *Teachers here are BIG petty.* My focus is back on her.

"Due to his extensive history of behavior incidents, including what he did today, I'm expelling him."

"You're what? So, you're going to put him out? And how is my son supposed to get an education? You're supposed to care about kids."

"I do care about kids, including Divine, which is why we are not going to press charges on him for today's fire."

"Whatever. Don't do me any favors."

She replied, "I'm not. This is to help Divine. It is my professional opinion that Divine could benefit from an evaluation. It can identify what help he might need. We would have arranged it, but you declined." She looked like she was carefully crafting that statement. It doesn't matter because it pissed me off.

"Yep, cuz ya'll not about to try to say my son is crazy so y'all can put him on medication."

"That's not exactly how the process works."

"I know how it is. My sister is a principal too. I also know schools get more money for kids labeled as special ed. It's all a big money grab for these schools."

"Extra funding helps secure more resources to support the students."

"Yeah right. I was not going to let y'all slap a label on my son. Ain't nothing wrong with Divine. He can be a little hard headed sometimes but that's all kids, especially boys."

"As his parent, how you decide to proceed is up to you."

"Tell me something I don't know."

"He appears to have a lot of anger in him and struggles with discipline. He becomes defiant."

"I've heard enough. This is for the best. I need to pull him out of here. He deserves to be at a school where he's encouraged instead of targeted."

"I have to make decisions in the best interest of everyone in this school. I wish Divine all the best. He's an intelligent young man. I would hate to see him cause severe damage to property or worse yet, do something to hurt himself or someone else."

"There's no need to worry about him because he's fine. Divine would never do anything to hurt anyone." *Maybe he did something to Legend's puppy (and I still wasn't sure about that). That's a damn dog, not a person.*

Little did I know, her words would come back to haunt me.

MAJESTY
Help

"Hey Maj, call me when you get off."

I don't know what she wants but I know she must need a favor or something which explains this voicemail.

"Hello."

"Hey Granny, What you doing girl?"

"Hey baby. I'm watching the news. You heard about that little girl that jumped on her teacher?"

"I don't know. It happens all the time now. These kids are out of control."

"That's what I know. That never happened in my day, cuz the whole family would beat that girl. What you want child? I need to get back to my program."

"Have you talked to Elegance today? She left me a message to call her. I thought maybe she already talked to you."

"Seems to me if you want to know why she called, you would call her and find out."

"Granny," I pleaded.

"She ain't call me and right now I wish you didn't either. Now Bye."

CLICK

I know she didn't hang up on me. Oh, I'm gonna get her. The next time she calls me because she doesn't remember how to work her DVR, I'm gonna do her the same way. I turn on the radio to my 90s R&B playlist, skipping ahead to my favorite slow jam by SWV. I listen to my jam to clear my mind and enjoy the drive home.

INCOMING CALL from Elegance.

Why is she stalking me?

INCOMING CALL from Elegance.

I don't feel like talking to her right now.

"Hey," I answer against my better judgment.

She replied with her usual attitude, "I know you saw me calling you."

"I'm sorry you don't understand I can't lolly gag on the phone while I'm at work. What's up?"

"I need your help."

I knew it. "Help with what?"

"Can you believe his school put him out?"

Yes, I can believe it. Nobody is shocked, but you. "What did he do?"

"She claims he set a fire in the bathroom."

"You're lucky they're not pressing charges."

"Now you sound like her. Maj, be his auntie right now instead of a principal."

"I know you don't want to hear this but you should take him to talk to someone. He has to learn how to process his emotions in a safe way."

"I literally just said be his auntie in this moment."

"So, you called to tell me he got kicked out of school?"

"Yes and..."

"And what?"

"And I need you to let him come to your school?"

"For what?"

"To be a damn student, that's for what. My baby doesn't deserve to go to an alternative school with all those bad ass kids."

He's one of those bad ass kids. He'd fit right in. "That sure sounds like a request for a principal, not an auntie." I wait for her response. "Huh? Did you say something?"

"Don't nobody have time for your games Majesty."

"I don't know about this. I can't have him causing a ruckus at my school."

"That's a damn shame. You automatically assume the worse."

"Save the drama, don't act like he doesn't stay getting in trouble."

"Of course he does when they target him. They've been calling me nonstop since last year. That's why half the time I ignore their calls and I blocked their emails."

"You ever consider working with them instead of against them? Schools need parents to partner with them."

"There's the principal again."

"I'm going to take one for the team. He can come. If he starts the foolishness I will put him out too. This is my job."

"This is my son, your nephew."

"If my staff recommends an evaluation, you have to consent to it."

"Fine. I'll bring him tomorrow. I can't keep missing all this time off from work and he needs to be in school."

"Don't expect any special treatment."

"Did I ask for that? I gotta go. Bye."

CLICK

"YOU COULD'VE SAID THANK YOU." I should call her back to say that. This whole call was about special treatment.

Wait til I tell Granny what she wanted. Lord, help me. How am I gonna tell Jayvon?

An hour later I'm in the kitchen putting the finishing touches on dinner. I made steak and potatoes with asparagus and dinner rolls. I need to butter Jayvon up with his favorite meal before I let him know what I agreed to.

He enters the kitchen. "Hey love." His lips are gentle as they press against mine.

"Hi baby."

"Hi Momma." Legend squeezes my waist.

"Hi sweetie. How was school?"

"Good."

"Go get washed up for dinner." Legend disappears upstairs.

"To what do I owe the honors?" Jayvon stares at me waiting for an answer.

"What? Nothing. I can't make my man's favorite meal?" I avoid his stare.

"Girl, I know you too well. What's up?"

"Let's enjoy dinner and we'll talk afterwards once Legend goes to sleep."

Dinner was great. Legend talked nonstop about martial arts and his upcoming role in his school play. He gets it honest from me and my momma (God bless the dead). After dinner, we played Connect Four and Uno before Legend did his nightly reading. He'd been in bed for 30 minutes or so.

"What's up?" Jayvon sat behind me on the bed.

"You know how important family is to me." I take a deep breath and release it slowly before continuing. "Elegance needed my help today."

"Help how?"

I explain how Divine was put out of school for setting the fire.

"I'm still waiting to hear how she needed your help."

"She asked if Divine could come to my school." I wait for his response.

"What did she say when you said no?" Now he's waiting for my response.

"Baby, I said yes."

He jumps up off the bed. "Majesty, please tell me you're joking. It's not your job to fix her problems with him." He's pacing back and forth.

"Baby, I can't turn my back on them. At least this way I can keep an eye on him." I plead with my eyes. *I need him to understand.*

"No you can't, but tell yourself that lie if you want. We both know it's not true."

"I understand your concerns."

"I don't think you do, Majesty. This is going to become a problem for you, which becomes a problem for me."

"Let's be positive."

"I'm being real. Keep it 100. You know he's going to do something that lands him in your office. This will create more tension between you and Elegance." He continues pacing. "If he didn't come to your school, where would he go?"

"Alternative school."

"That's where he belongs."

"It's rough there."

"Of course it is because it's where the kids with awful behavior go. The kids who are given chance after chance but still don't change. The kids who commit criminal acts are usually rough. Divine set a fire at school, he's rough."

"Jayvon, It's complicated."

He shakes his head side to side. "It's not. You all can't shield him from the consequences of his actions. Actually, that's exactly what y'all are doing but you shouldn't."

He rejoins me on the bed. "Sometimes when you believe you're helping someone, you're instead hurting them. Elegance enables his behavior and now you're enabling hers." He pulls my hand into his large hand.

"He might be at your school now but I don't want him over here all the time. Legend needs to keep a healthy distance away from him."

I nod in agreement.

"Majesty, I'm serious about this."

"Alright," I release my hand and massage my temples.

"I hate to say it but Divine is going to end up in prison with his dad or buried next to your mother."

ELEGANCE

Questions

You have a lot of explaining to do. How do you explain yourself? Did you do it? I'm rehearsing the best way to approach the conversation over dinner. Divine and I made it home, we were eating his favorite meal - pizza and wings.

"What happened at school today?"

"Nothing," he shrugs his shoulders.

"What happened in the bathroom?"

"I took a piss...Ha Ha Ha".

I slam my hand on the table. "Divine, stop playing with me. What did you do?"

"I don't know what you're talking about." His facial expression blank.

"I'm talking about the fire you set."

"What about it? I'm sure that bitch at school told you everything."

"I want to hear from you."

"Too bad cuz I don't wanna talk about it."

"Who do you think you're talking to?"

He jumps up and walks up on me while clenching his fist.

He's so close to me, making the room feel small.

My breathing feels shallow.

"I'm talking to you. You're gonna learn to leave me alone."

"You better get out my face and stop playing with me."

"Or what? What you gonna do?"

"Nothing cuz you better do what I said."

He takes his time backing up before sitting back down.

His eyes still fixed on me.

"You have to stop doing all this dumb shit before these people try to put you on meds or send you away somewhere. I may not be able to always protect you. You need to listen to me."

"I know what Auntie and Uncle think about me. In a minute they're gonna turn Legend against me and probably you too."

"We all love you and I would never turn against you."

"I don't care if you do. It's me versus everybody."

"Don't say that. You always got me. You know that."

"I don't know nothing. Your boyfriend probably gonna make you hate me. I know bruh don't like me."

"That's not true, Darvin likes you."

"Ew bruh sound sus."

"What does that mean?"

"Damn, you don't know nothing. That sounds suspect."

"Don't say that."

"I can say what I want. Maybe I'll tell my counselor that when I go back to school."

"Tell them what?"

"How my momma's boyfriend likes me a lot. He always gives me gifts. You know what I mean, right?" He's smirking at me.

"Don't joke like that."

"Who says I'm joking?"

"It's not cool to lie on people."

"I can if I want to."

"You shouldn't."

"I don't care. How long do I gotta stay home this time?"

"You're not staying home. She put you out so now you're going to your Auntie's school."

"I ain't going there."

"Oh, yes you are."

"I bet I skip everyday. Watch."

"If you don't go to school I can get in trouble. Is that what you want?"

He stares at me without a trace of any emotion.

"You're scared of getting in trouble? Not me?" He smiles.

"Whatever," I stand up. "You're going to her school."

He stands up too. "You already said that." He's nodding to himself. "I can't wait to meet my new counselor. What would happen to you if...? Never mind, I'll ask the counselor. I got a lot to say, one day soon ya'll gonna listen to me."

"Fine. Ok. You can stay home tomorrow but you're going on Friday." He grabs the box of pizza and heads to his room. BAM. He slams his bedroom door.

Ugh-Teenagers. Guess I'm only eating wings since he's claimed the pizza. He has a weird sense of humor, like his dad. Everybody talked shit about his daddy and his people. I won't let my son feel isolated like he did. He can have his day to get his mind right before going to his new school.

This shit has worn me out. I retreat to my room. I pour a glass of my favorite red wine. I slip into my jacuzzi tub allowing the jets and bubbles to provide a much needed massage. The slight vanilla scent from my candle hangs in the air. I lean back on my bath pillow and close my eyes. This type of peace often escapes me. What will it take to have this all the time? I need all the craziness to stop. This calm environment has me slipping away. I won't fight it. After my soothing experience in the tub, I'm in my bed in a deep sleep.

I shouldn't have drank all that wine. I turn to see the clock on my nightstand. The blue numbers show *it's 4:16 a.m. There's no way I can hold it until my alarm goes off at 6:00 a.m.*

"Oh, Hey Divine."

"DIVINE!" I holler and turn on my lamp. "What the hell are you doing in my room in the middle of the night?"

"I heard you yelling."

As my eyes get adjusted to the low glow from the lamp, I see my son standing in the middle of my bedroom floor. His expression looks different, unfamiliar. "I wasn't yelling. I was sleep." He shrugs his shoulders. The movement brings my attention to his hands and that's when I see it.

"Why do you have a butcher knife?"

He remains silent.

"Answer me."

He mumbles, "It's for protection."

"Protection—

From what?"

Where'd you get it?

You shouldn't have a knife."

I tell him to bring it to me. He opens his hand allowing the knife to fall out, never once flinching. Divine turns and walks out my room.

I race to close my door, my hand shaking as I lock it. I attempt to steady my hand as I hide the knife in my nightstand. Where did he get this from? I don't recognize it from my kitchen set.

I rush to use the bathroom, peeing as fast as I can, my leg shaking nonstop. The peace I experienced a few hours ago is replaced by anxiety. I double check the lock on my door before climbing back in bed. I'm wondering why I feel so uneasy as I try to slow down my rapid breathing.

Maybe I was yelling, I consider.

He probably did come to check on me.

I guess it makes sense he'd come in armed.

There's no other reason...right?

I jump out of bed and grab a chair to place against my door, checking the lock again.

I can't shake the question...How many other secret weapons does Divine have that I don't know about?

MAJESTY

Peace

"Hey baby how did it go?"

"He hasn't come yet Granny." I explained how Elegance said Divine would start fresh on Monday.

"That's likely for the best, no need to rush trouble. Enjoy your peace."

"I pray he doesn't cause trouble at my school because I'd never hear the end of it from Jayvon. I would have to hide it from him."

"I don't get involved in married folks business but you know you shouldn't hide things from your husband. The Lord won't bless that."

I roll my eyes, happy that Granny couldn't see it. "I know, I just want to help Divine without making Jayvon upset."

"Baby, have you seen my piece?"

"No, why?"

"I can't seem to find it. I must have moved it and don't remember where I put it."

"Are you sure, Granny?"

"I'm sure Chile, I switched my pocketbook and must have hid it from myself."

"Make sure you find it, let me know if you don't. I'll let you go so I can finish up on this work and get home to make dinner since Jayvon is out of town. Talk to you later. Love you."

After hanging up with Granny, I talk to Elegance.

"I got you Maj, especially after how you helped us."

"I appreciate it. I should only be here another hour or two."

"Take your time. I'll get some dinner. It's been a minute since the boys hung out, it'll be good for them to kick it."

"Please keep your eyes on them."

"Stop worrying so much, ain't nothing gonna happen."

I thank her again and end the call with a smile on my face. It felt good to be on good terms with her. Like Granny said, I'm going to enjoy my peace.

I return to my never ending to-do list. I love my job but sometimes the lines get blurred between work life and home life. Often home gets short-changed.

Soon... home will demand all my attention.

ELEGANCE
Bitch

"Go on and eat."

"Thanks Auntie."

"You're welcome baby." *Legend was always respectful.*

"We're going to my room to chill. C'mon Legend."

"Bye Auntie." Legend waved.

I love how the boys love each other despite the issues Majesty and I have sometimes. We used to be close like that but Ms. Goody Two Shoes started acting like she was my momma so I had to show her, she wasn't. Since the boys are hanging out and doing their thing, I decide to get caught up on my favorite show on OWN. Those couples know they keep up so much drama and I'm here for it.

Lately I've been dealing with my own drama with my man always talking trash about my son. Let me holler at him real quick.

> So u just gonna ghost me?????

> I told u we need to chill 4 a minute

> How long is a minute?????

EBONY Q.

IDK... as long as I need... as long as it takes

U can't be serious—U really trippin over my son? Kids are bad, especially lil boys.

Divine is bad as hell and u refuse to believe it... U living a lie

Don't talk about my son cuz U AIN'T PERFECT

I can't do this with u. I'ma come get my stuff and bring u ya key. FRFR u should get him some help before shit gets worse.

FUCK U!!! Divine was right, u act like a lil bitch. My tissue harder than you.

Don't hit my line no more. Good luck with ya psycho ass son cuz he's gonna end up wearing orange or he's gonna have u wearing black. U can bet that up. U think the shit he does is cute but wait until he turns on u. U gonna see who the real bitch is.

MAJESTY

Sorry

BZZZ BZZZ BZZZ.

I look at my phone vibrating on my desk. *What does she want? I'll call her back in a minute. I'm almost done.*

BZZZ BZZZ BZZZ.

Why is she blowing my phone up? I'll call her in a little bit when I get in the car.

CLICK CLACK CLICK CLACK CLICK CLACK. The sound of my keyboard is so satisfying as I complete the items on my checklist. I beam with pride

BZZZ BZZZ BZZZ.

Not again! She's being a bug-a-boo. I glance down at my phone and to my surprise I see Jayvon's picture. He must be calling to check in.

"Hey baby."

He's screaming into the phone I can't make out what he's saying.

"Jay, I can't understand you. What's wrong?"

"I TOLD YOU KEEP LEGEND AWAY FROM DIVINE. I TOLD YOU—

"What's wrong?"

"Legend is being rushed to the hospital. There was an accident at Elegance's house. Get your ass to the hospital ASAP!"

CLICK.

He ends the call.

I grab my phone and purse and run out the building. I was so focused on finishing my work that I'd almost forgotten that Legend was at her house.

What accident?

My damn dog still hadn't recovered from his accident.

I fly to the hospital, my thoughts bouncing all over the place like the ball in a pinball machine.

"Call Elegance," I command to my car. The phone rings and then her voicemail picks up. I hang up.

"Call Elegance," I command again but get the same results. Before I can give the command again I receive an incoming call. I answer immediately.

"Hey baby," Gran's voice fills the speakers in my small car.

"Have you talked to Elegance? What accident? Is Legend ok?" I fired off my questions not allowing Grandma to answer.

"I spoke to her a few minutes ago. They just got to the ER. I'm on the way too. I said my prayers before I left."

"What happened?

How's Legend?

Is he ok?"

"I don't know. She said they rushed him into surgery. Hurry and get there. I gotta go so I can drive. I'll see you after while."

I arrive to the hospital, barely putting the car in park before sprinting inside.

Elegance approaches me, "Majesty I'm -

"THIS IS YOUR FAULT," I slap the dog piss out of her, sending her hoop earring to the floor.

"OOOWW—

I cut off her screaming by grabbing her neck, squeezing as tight as I can, digging my nails into her flesh. I'm trying to squeeze the life out of her, staring into her bulging eyes. Her attempts to free herself are no match for my rage fueled strength. I'm pulled from behind. Someone else is pulling at my hands. The security guards are trying to rip me off her. They're able to get me off and put space between us.

"Majesty, I'm sorry. It was an accident. They were playing." She rubbed her face.

"Stay away from me. It's a good thing I don't see Divine here either or I'd beat his ass like you need to."

"It was an accident."

"Go to hell. You and him are dead to me."

ELEGANCE
Accident

I didn't leave the hospital. Majesty said some messed up stuff but I know she's angry and scared, she doesn't mean what she said. I understand where she's coming from, which is why I didn't beat her ass for putting her hands on me.

Gran finally arrived. I felt some type of way that she went to check on Majesty first. She always liked her better than me. I'm watching them talk and steal glances at me. If looks could kill I'd be dead from how Majesty was shooting daggers my way. *I don't need this bullshit. I'm leaving.*

I stand up to leave. The doctor comes in to give me an update.

"Don't you dare talk to her. I'm his mother." Majesty says.

"I'm sorry, I know he arrived with her."

"As I stated, I'm his mother."

"Yes Ma'am. He acknowledges. "He's still in critical condition, there's a tremendous amount of internal damage, scarring. We had to put him in a medically induced coma to allow his lungs to recover. He sustained a great deal of damage there."

"But he's going to survive, right?" Majesty's eyes are pleading for the answer she wants, but it's not the answer she gets.

"We're doing our best but he's not out of the clear yet." The doctor promises to return as soon as there's another update.

"Ms. Elegance Patterson?" A man in a tired suit asks.

"Yes?"

"I'm Detective Hines and this is Detective Craig," he gestured to the middle aged woman with him. "We need to ask you some questions about the accident." They stare at me. "It was an accident, right?"

"Of course it was."

The female detective asks, "What exactly happened? Start from the beginning and don't leave anything out." She has her pen positioned on a little pad, waiting to capture my side of the story.

I explain how the boys wanted to hang out in Divine's room. They were eating and having a good time. I kept checking in on them to make sure they weren't getting into anything. *I didn't but they don't know that.* I'd left out the room because my phone rang.

"Who called you?"

Why does it matter? Damn she's nosey. "It was my boyfriend."

"We'll need his name and number. Can you show me in your call log?"

"My phone is dead so I can't show you that right now." *They're not slick. I see them cut their eyes to each other. I hate cops. I see my Grandma and Majesty cut their eyes to each other too. They've turned this into me against them.*

"After talking to him for a few minutes, I went to check on the boys again. That's when I noticed my nephew on the floor, clenching his throat in a puddle of vomit."

"And what was your son doing?"

"He was standing there panicked."

"I see," she scribbled on her little pad. "What did your son say happened?"

"They were playing a game and Legend got sick."

"Game? What type of game?"

"Right, that's what I want to know." Majesty said.

I tell them it was a social media challenge. All the kids on Video Book were posting videos of the super clean challenge.

"Oh no," Majesty whines.

"What's wrong baby?" Gran asks.

The detective explains the super clean challenge. It's where kids pour household cleaners in each other's mouth. The challenge is to see how long you can hold it without swallowing or spitting it out.

The male detective asks, "Where is your son, Divine?"

DIVINE

Boss

My mama told me to take the video down.
But I didn't.
I had three thousand views and counting. Before the ambulance came she told me to get rid of the cups and chemicals. I hid it all. She kept blowing up my phone, texting, asking if I did it. I finally answered and said yes. Hours later she returned home and we both left to head to the police station.

We went in a room in the back. It looks like the rooms on TV with a table and chairs. I notice there's a camera in the ceiling. Two detectives come in. The man tells me to tell him everything that happened. I stare at him. He repeats himself. I stare and shake my head side to side.

"Would you feel more comfortable if your mother stepped out?"

I shake my head up and down. My mama looks surprised.

"Do you mind stepping out?" He asks mama.

Mama and the lady leave out but then the lady comes back.

"Go ahead and tell us about the accident."

The thought of my views and likes...

Has me turnt up.

My page gonna be lit.

EBONY Q.

"Number 1, I'm a boss."
"Number 2, It wasn't no accident."

ELEGANCE
Shocked

The detectives return to the room I'm waiting in.

"Can we go now? I need to get back to the hospital with my family."

"Divine is under arrest."

"What? I shouldn't have let him talk to y'all. What did y'all say to my baby?"

"He confessed to everything." *They smirk at each other.*

"Bull shit. What did y'all make him say?"

"See for yourself." They put a laptop on the table and press play.

I watch Divine's confession in shock. "He's not telling the truth. He's making that up."

"Tell it to the judge." The female detective opens the door, a uniformed officer comes in holding handcuffs. "Elegance Patterson, you're under arrest for aiding and abetting a minor, contributing to the delinquency of a minor, and child abuse."

"What?" I question. "Y'all are wrong."

"Your son told us everything. You saw the video. You helped him by providing the chemicals and you helped try to cover it up."

"That's not true. He's lying."

"We saw the messages on his phone. We recovered the chemicals and cups used and we saw the post he made. You're *in* the post. Your son also had a nice collection of weapons. Why does he have a gun and knives?"

" A gun and knives...What?"

"Some kind of mother you are," the female detective spat "Don't act shocked now. You should be ashamed of yourself." She frowned at me.

"He is lying.

—He never tells the truth.

—Ask anybody."

"I guess he gets his truthfulness from you. We talked to your *ex*-boyfriend. He said he didn't call you. Why'd you lie about that?"

"I didn't lie. I got confused."

"There's a preponderance of evidence against both of you."

"I'm innocent.

—My son did this, not me.

—He's troubled, you gotta believe me."

"Looks like your next family reunion will be in prison. Get her out of here." The uniform officer had me stand and placed the cuffs on me.

Tears start streaming down my face faster than a raging river.

I should've listened to everyone.

How could my baby do this to me?

I would've never believed Divine would turn on me...

Not like this.

Not my son.

MAJESTY
Betrayal

The past seven months have been rough. My family had to lay our loved one to rest. He fought as long as he could. Looking back, I can't help but feel like this was all my fault and I should've listed to Jayvon.

We'll never be the same.

RIP Rocky.

We'll miss you, especially Legend.

Legend is still recovering. He suffered severe internal burns and scarring from the bleach and ammonia he ingested. He sees a counselor to help him deal with the emotional wounds. I'm seeing a therapist now to help me cope with everything.

Jayvon left me. It broke my heart to have him look at me with such disgust. He said he didn't trust me or my judgement, especially when it came to Elegance and Divine. He hasn't filed for a divorce so I believe there's a chance we can get past this and get back together. I want that more than anything, for him to move back into our home and be a family again.

I didn't help Elegance or Divine with their legal fees. She begged me to but I refused. Part of me felt like I was turning my back on them for saying no. I had to realize they're in that situation due to their actions and it's not my responsibility to rescue them.

Granny said she was proud of me. I was proud of me too. For once I put *my* family first. I knew Jayvon was watching closely to see how I handled the situation.

Granny has tried to remain strong through all this but I can tell it's wearing on her. She never liked us being at odds. In the blink of an eye, she lost two of her family members to incarceration. She's visited them both a time or two. I refuse to go see them, accept the collect calls or letters, or put money on their books. They're living the life they chose.

Granny said I wouldn't recognize Divine because he grew his hair out and has tattoos all over his arms and neck. Divine is happy behind bars. He believes that's where he's supposed to be, like his father. He said he feels more love in there from his boys than he did when he was with us. Granny said he sounds plum crazy and I agree. It low-key bothered me that he feels that way.

We did our best with him.

His mother was his biggest supporter — to a fault.

My fault was being loyal to my sister instead of my husband.

Loyalty betrayed us all.

Thanks for reading! You're now a #EQReader. Please help me out & leave a review. Include the hashtag in your review.

EXCLUSIVES

Sign-up for my email list to receive Ebony Q. Exclusives. Be the first to find out what I'm working on. I won't spam you or share your info. You can unsubscribe at anytime.

Join my journey here: https://www.authorebonyq.com

Want to keep the story going? Get behind the scenes story info, like story inspiration and hear directly from the characters with interviews.

Get more info at https://www.authorebonyq.com/blog

ALSO BY EBONY Q.

N'Dea is a self-proclaimed party girl. Each weekend you can find her in the club with her girls, having the time of her life. Young & carefree, N'Dea is ignorant to the shady characters in the club who hide in plain sight.

One night N'Dea becomes a target. Someone's been watching her, hoping to catch her slipping. If N'Dea sticks to her usual party ways, she'll live to talk about it. If she strays, she'll learn secrets of a dangerous meaning for "party girl," but who can she tell?

Get a free copy here: https://www.authorebonyq.com

DISCUSSION/REFLECTION QUESTIONS

Use for a book club or reflection

1. What was your favorite or least favorite part of the book?
2. Which scene has stuck with you the most?
3. Did you reread any passages? If so, which one?
4. Would you want to read another book by this author?
5. Did reading the book impact your mood? If yes, how so?
6. What surprised you most about the book?
7. Did the book's title match the book's contents? If you could give the book a new title, what would it be?
8. Are there lingering questions from the book you're still thinking about?
9. Did the book strike you as original?
10. How did you feel about the ending? Was it satisfying or did you want more?
11. How did the author keep you interested or surprised throughout the story?
12. What was the most memorable or shocking scene or twist in the story and why?
13. Are there any characters you wish you could have given advice to? What would you tell them?

DISCUSSION/REFLECTION QUESTIONS

14. What do you think happens to the characters after the novel concludes?
15. Share a favorite quote from the book. Why did this quote stand out?
16. Did this book seem realistic?
17. Did the characters seem believable to you? Did they remind you of anyone?
18. Did the characters' motives seem reasonable or a little far-fetched?
19. How relevant or relatable are the themes or messages of the book to your own life, or to society today?
20. If you disagreed with Majesty or Elegance, what would you have done differently?
21. Did the family's relationships & interactions seem realistic?

Authors love to hear from their readers.
Share your response to one of the questions with the author. Go to
https://www.authorebonyq.com/contact

ABOUT THE AUTHOR

Ebony lives in Georgia. She has always loved to read urban fiction. She also enjoys watching true crime dramas. Ebony prides herself on writing fiction where real people, not characters, experience real-life situations. Her motto is "Telling our stories my way." **Please tag me in a social media post showing the book cover & quote your favorite line or share your thoughts. Use the hashtags #EQReader and #authorebonyq.**

- facebook.com/authorebonyq
- tiktok.com/@ebonyq02
- instagram.com/authorebonyq

Made in the USA
Columbia, SC
07 December 2023